THIS IS US NOW

Love in the time of cancer

Jacinta Dietrich

Grattan Street Press

THIS IS US NOW

Published by Grattan Street Press, 2021

Grattan Street Press is the imprint of the
teaching press based in the School of Culture and
Communication at the University of Melbourne,
Parkville, Australia.

THE UNIVERSITY OF
MELBOURNE

Cover image copyright © Grattan Street Press, 2021.
Author photography by Simon McCarthy.
Typeset in Adobe Bodoni.

Grattan Street Press
School of Culture and Communication
John Medley Building,
Parkville, VIC 3010
www.grattanstreetpress.com

Printed in Australia
ISBN: 9780648209652

A catalogue record for this book is available from the National Library
of Australia

To Lucas, for letting me mine our story for fictional gems.
It meant more than either of us could've anticipated.

Prologue

Why are all the cancer movies always the same? They're always stories about people who find love in the cancer ward and help each other through treatment. About first loves and first times and first losses.

Or the couple that has been together for decades only to have their love ravaged by illness. One is taken after a long battle and the other is left mourning.

Sometimes I'd like to see the couple in their mid-twenties trying to figure things out while their lives shift around them. The couple that met when they were both healthy and having fun and traded cocktails in bars for a cocktail of chemo drugs. The couple that balances meeting the parents with meeting the oncologist. The couple that learns their partner's Medicare number before their mobile.

Sometimes I want to see a story like ours.

Part I

Ella

We sit in the middle of Carlton Gardens. The Royal Exhibition Building looms above us, the sky blue and cloudless behind it. I can hear rushing cars, rushing trams, rushing water from the fountain. Everything moving around us. I'd normally be rushing with the rest of it – working, studying, hustling, speeding through my day. It's nice to be slow for a change.

Theo unpacks a feast – chunks of feta, slices of bread, sun-dried tomatoes, olives, salami. My mouth salivates. He looks at me. His eyes are swirls of brown and gold and full of affection. Normally it makes me uncomfortable, the adoration in his eyes, all his love blasting in a wave that crashes over me. But today it's special. Today I feel that special. I lean across and kiss him. His lips are soft. He tastes like warm black coffee.

'Happy anniversary,' I say. His eyes crinkle when he smiles.

'One year from a Tinder swipe,' he says. 'Not bad.'

'Not bad at all.' I chew on an olive and press it, smooth and salty, against my tongue. He's still looking at me with those gooey eyes. I open my mouth and show him what remains of the olive.

'Delightful,' he says, and laughs.

'You think we've got another year in us?' I ask.

'With all your class and all my patience, I'm sure we can manage it. Plus, we'll be stuck in a lease, so that's an incentive.'

In the weeks leading up to our next anniversary,

there will be talk of coming back here. But there will be too many fears about dirt and animals and airborne bacteria. We will be tired and scared, not willing to risk anything, let alone everything, on a picnic outside. Instead, I will pull out the rug and lay it out in the middle of his parents' living room. I will put out the food he can stomach – slices of white bread, bowls of hot chips, Minties, dark chocolate, ginger beer – and watch as he picks at them. His eyes will still be full of love, but they will also be red-rimmed and exhausted from the effort of being awake. When I kiss him, his lips will be dry and cracked. He will taste like salt and mouthwash.

*

I wait for Theo in the lounge room. He heads straight for the kitchen like it's his own home and flicks on the kettle. I can hear him rustling around, mugs and jars clanging against one another.

'Tea or coffee?' he calls out. Theo needs five coffees to get him through the day. The last time he went without coffee, he shouted at a cyclist, got on the wrong train line and locked himself out of the house.

'How about some bubbly?' I ask.

'I don't think you have any,' he calls back. My hint doesn't make a sound as it swoops straight over his head.

'I have news.'

His head pops around the wall.

'Oh my god. Am I pregnant? El, I'm so excited. I'm sure you're the father.' He waddles over to me, holding his stomach with his back arched. To his credit, he actually does a pretty convincing waddle. I can't help but laugh.

'No, you goose. You and I are going to be co-leasers.'

'The agent approved our application?'

'The agent approved our application. We move in a month. We can sign the lease on Friday.'

'You ready to cohabit with all o' this?' He gestures up and down, waving his arms like a casino showgirl. His hands rest on his hips as he sloppily belly dances his way around the living room, singing a mumbled version of Shakira's 'Hips Don't Lie'. I grab his hand and pull him into a hug. He holds me and we sway together, slow dancing to the rhythm of the boiling kettle.

'I'm so ready to cohabit with all this,' I say. ' Theo?'

'Yeah?'

I lean back a little so I can look into his eyes. 'Your baby's going to be beautiful. I don't think it's mine, but, you know what, I'll raise it as my own anyway.'

He laughs. We sway.

*

'Can I get you anything?' Theo asks, tossing his bag on top of the others and pulling out his basketball.

His fingers fit around its pimpled surface as he tosses it from one hand to the other. He's not even looking at it. 'There's a bottle of water in the bag if you need it,' he says. 'I also packed you some snacks 'cause I know you'll get hungry watching all this exercise.' He laughs and I stick out my tongue, but secretly I'm stoked.

'Man, had I known I'd get snacks I would've come to a game before now,' I tease. This time he sticks out his tongue. He's still tossing the ball without looking. His jersey slides over his muscles. I want to run my hands under his shirt and feel them. He leans in and pecks me on the cheek before running onto the court and tossing the ball straight into the hoop. He turns around and winks. Show-off.

The siren shrieks and the other players roll their balls off the court, take their positions and start running. Their shoes beat as they charge up and down, the rhythm syncopated with the thud of the ball against the court. Their rubber soles screech in my ears and the whistle squeals. Theo's legs pump as he runs, I can see the sweat shining on his skin. He definitely takes it more seriously than he let on. The ball flies across the court and Theo lunges for it.

The elbow comes out of nowhere, colliding with the side of his head. His body keeps moving forward but his head is halted by the impact. There is a sickening thud as he hits the floor. Seconds pass. He doesn't move. His team rush to his side. The ref calls for a timeout. Theo finally groans and I breathe again. His teammates urge him to stay still – they've all heard the horror stories of broken necks and broken backs on the court. He shrugs them off. He tries to stand, but only manages to sit up. Drops of blood from the back of his head have been smeared onto the polished floor. He runs his fingers through his hair and groans again. They come away red. I can see it from here, sticking to his fingers and in his hair.

The first aider runs over to him but he waves her away. He stands and stretches, groans again. He shuffles over to me. I'm already collecting tissues and bandaids and anything else I can find in the bags around me. The game resumes. I press the tissues against his head to stem the oozing blood, before peeling them back to take a look. The cut doesn't seem long or deep but the blood is surging with his pulse, spurting out red waves with every heartbeat. The first aider hovers near us and nods at my handiwork. I get Theo's hand and make him hold the tissues in place, then stomp around the seats fetching his things and shoving them roughly into his bag.

'Babe, settle down,' he says.

'You could've been seriously hurt.' My teeth are tight. 'What if you landed differently? What if you broke something? What if you broke your neck?' More scenarios roll through my head but I can't verbalise them. What would I do if he was seriously injured? I don't even want to think about it.

'Ella, you're being dramatic. It's fine. Just a cut.'

'I am not being dramatic. That could've been really serious.' I look at his wide brown eyes. He is watching me collect his things, a smirk on his face. I can't help but soften.

'But it wasn't. A near miss is still a miss. I'm okay. Really.'

I come back to inspect the cut, showing the first aider over my shoulder. The bleeding has slowed now that his pulse has settled. It is just a small cut after all, won't even need stitches. 'You sure?' I ask, the question meant for both of them. The first aider nods before going back to watch the game from her place in the stand. Relief floods through me. Theo tugs me into a one-armed hug. I move my arms around his neck and my body fits snugly between his knees. He smells of sweat and laundry powder and him.

*

'What'll you do when you finish uni?' he asks.

His hands move over mine as he weaves our fingers together. I feel heat from his body next to me, and the pillow soft and cool on my neck. The 3 p.m. sun seeps through my window, covering everything in a warm glow.

'I dunno,' I reply. 'Eat. Read. Sleep in. Give myself a bit of a break. Then get an adult job when I can. Guess it just depends on who will hire me.'

I see myself sitting at a desk, fitted blazer hanging

off the back of the chair, doing the 8 a.m.–7 p.m. grind that everyone thinks is normal. I cross my fingers that I'll get lucky, end up in a cool, creative job, something where I can actually use my arts degree in more satisfying ways than writing copy for products people don't need. Though right now anything sounds better than working at a cinema. Everyone thinks it's the coolest job when they ask where I work – they want to know about free movie tickets, discounted popcorn and if I get to watch the movies before release. But mostly it's cooking popcorn, selling popcorn and then cleaning spilled popcorn. And when it's not, it's explaining that you don't control the price of tickets or forcing a smile for the hundredth time when you ask a customer where they would like to sit and they say, 'preferably in the cinema'. School holidays are coming and I can't handle finding one more dirty nappy shoved under the seats or cleaning another kid's vomit while the parent looks on apologetically (or, in some cases, not even bothering with that courtesy).

'What're you gonna do?' I ask.

'I want to travel,' he says. 'I want to see all the parts of this world I haven't seen yet. I want to explore.'

'Where do you want to go?'

'Everywhere,' he says. 'Wherever there are buildings, I want to see them. Barcelona for Gaudi's, Paris for the Gothics, Agra for the Taj Mahal. But also the food. I want to eat sauerbraten in Germany and a real Moroccan tagine. I want to taste Guinness in

Dublin and champagne in Champagne.'

He keeps talking. The sun is shining on his face as he sits up. The light makes his eyes gleam and his mouth turns up slightly at the edges, a dreamy smile as he talks. His face is as clear as the map he is describing, everything he's thinking visible in the shape of his mouth, his eyes and brow.

'But I want to end up in London, live there a year or two,' he says.

'Why London?' I ask.

'The architecture mainly. There's beautiful architecture everywhere, but there's more of London I want to explore. Plus, the dream job with the dream architectural firm is in London, not that I expect to move over and land a job with them, obviously. But I felt at home when I visited London. I thought, "I could live here," and there aren't many other places I've felt that.'

I imagine him in London, rugged up in a scarf, coat and beanie, sitting in a cafe while he draws up his designs. He would draw the cafes around him and the ones in his head, the sketches rough and messy before moving on to his bolder designs – the restaurants with rooftop terrace gardens or beautiful libraries with intricate woodwork. He would grow the beard he keeps talking about, thick and bushy. My heart lurches a little. Will we stay together if he moves to London?

'Do you want to come with me?' he asks.

'Want to come with you where?'

'To London.'

'You want me to come live with you? In London?'

'Well, yeah, why not?' He shuffles a little beside me, his cheeks flushing. His eyes are staring at our intertwined hands.

My pulse throbs and my veins feel like they are going to burst. A thrill runs through my body, goosebumps chase across my skin. I try to imagine us in London. Both of us in scarves and coats and beanies. Both of us sitting in cafes, working on our projects. He would be drawing, I would be writing. We would have a regular cafe with a regular spot and a regular order. They would know our names. He would point out buildings and bridges, I would point out libraries and bookshops. I am swept up in the dream of it all, before I burst the bubble myself. Will we still be together in a year or two? Could I pick up my life and leave? Would I do that for him, for us? How am I meant to know that? But still, the idea sends an excited shiver through me. Maybe I could.

'Fuck,' he mutters. 'It's too soon to ask that. Way too soon.' It spills out of his mouth, the words tumbling one after the other. 'Fuck's sake. Sorry. Forget it, forget I said anything. Too much pressure. Sorry.'

I can see it in his eyes, the fear of being stuck, of saying something and not being able to unsay it. I can't help it – I start laughing. Big, belly-deep, tears-in-my-eyes laughter.

'You probably think I'm totally crazy now,' he says.

I give his hand a little squeeze. 'I would love to live

in London with you.'

*

I wait for him, standing in the alcove snuggled into the heritage brick wall, hidden away from wind and sight. I can hear the train clunking along the tracks, a thunderous sound rolling overhead. I close my eyes, listening to the rhythm. *Duh-dunk duh-dunk duh-dunk.* The brakes squeak as the carriages slow, giving a final screech when the train stops. It will take him only a few moments to walk down the ramp and look for me, but I'm not willing to leave the warmth of my alcove just yet. I've forgotten to bring a jumper and my arms are covered in goosebumps.

Wind sweeps through the walkway, scattering leaves and empty wrappers in its wake. The train horn blares and the carriages roll off to their next destination. *Duh-dunk duh-dunk duh-dunk.* I feel the cold, rough brick against my back and wait for the sounds of shuffling feet rushing down the ramp. I see the first trickle of people. They pull their coat collars up and tighten their scarves against the cold.

I hear him before I see him, his basketball shoes thump against the concrete. His footfalls echo over the others, a steady rhythm against the click of heels and clatter of dress shoes. When he comes into view, I smile. His pace quickens when he can't see me waiting, his head flicking from side to side as he looks up and down the tunnel. It makes the top of his beanie flop in all different directions and I laugh. He stops walking and searches his pockets for his phone. People flow down the ramp around him, like water streaming around a rock. Some frown as they pass.

I enjoy watching him when he is distracted. Theo doesn't have the same sense that other people do – that sense that he is being watched. If he is doing something, he is giving it one hundred per cent of his attention and often misses the bigger picture. He never turns around at parties when my eyes are searing into the back of his skull. He doesn't turn around now.

I stick my head past the row of bricks and whistle. His head turns, his eyes searching for the familiar noise. He smiles and moves towards me, his long legs building to a clumsy, enthusiastic skip. I stifle a laugh. His grin widens and his skip becomes even more ridiculous. Sometimes I wonder if he knows what he looks like.

His body is warm against mine as he presses into the alcove to kiss me.

'Aren't you cold?' he says, tugging at the sleeve of his jumper, pulling it up and over his head in one smooth movement. 'Chuck this on.'

I drag the oversized jumper on, feeling the soft wool as my fingers slide through the sleeve. It comes down to my thighs, but I don't mind. I look at him and hold the bottom of the jumper and do a little curtsy. He smiles and stretches out his arms for another hug.

'What's that?' I ask. A thin bandage is wrapped around his left elbow, folding into the crease.

'Nothing.' He pulls his arms back, trying to shield it, but I reach out to stop him. He winces as I grab hold. Too tight. I lessen the pressure but keep my hand gently resting on the bandage. He removes my grip and lifts my hand to his lips. He kisses my fingers one by one, a peck for each knuckle.

'I just got a test. No big deal.'

'Is everything okay?'

'Yeah, it's fine. Just a check-up. Nothing to worry about. All good. Super healthy.' He flexes his arms like a bodybuilder, turning his wrists this way and that as he arches his chest and tenses his biceps. Despite his reassurances, my eyes still follow the bandage. He traces his fingers across the lines on my forehead.

'You stress too much. Now, are we gonna race or not?'

We had agreed to race home. I am a mess of activewear. My white and pink shoes clash against my olive tights, and my singlet underneath his jumper declares my unironic love of kale. I know I look stupid, but I don't care.

We walk out of the station, the wind beating against our bodies. I press my arm against him, my hand in his. As we walk, our bodies fall into step together, each adjusting for the other without us noticing.

'So, first person to the apartment door is the winner?' he asks.

'Seems fair. But you've got to keep your backpack on,' I say. 'And I get a ten-second head start.' My eyes search the terrain for any more advantages. 'And I get to take the inside line on any corners.'

'Sure,' he laughs. 'And when I win, do I get to choose dinner or the movie?' He grins.

'When I win, I'll be choosing both.' I know what he would choose: an old classic film I've never heard of, which he would fall asleep halfway through, with Singapore noodles and special fried rice. I would choose an animated feature with at least three musical numbers, cheap pizza and cheesy garlic bread.

He drops his hand and starts to stretch his arms as we walk. I know I have no chance of winning, but I've bragged too much to give the game away now. Most of our competitions are based on me getting too far in and being too competitive to give up. Sometimes I even win by chance.

I start to quicken my pace. He knows this means I'm adding crucial seconds to my head start. He lets me get a few steps in front and when I turn back, he's smirking.

'Well, go on then. Your ten seconds starts now. You better run fast,' he says. I race off. I can hear him loudly counting the seconds behind me.

'Seven. Eight. Nine. Nine and a half. Nine and three quarters.' Then just the sound of his shoes pounding against the concrete behind me. I push harder as his footsteps gain momentum, my muscles tighten with the effort.

He is the superior athlete. I know that. Years of swimming and basketball have transformed his muscles into speed-producing machinery. He still goes running every morning before work to keep his body in the habit. He hikes on weekends. If I'm being completely honest, physical activities rest on the lower end of my priorities. It shows. I can count my running experiences on one hand, two if I'm lucky. The last time I went running I nearly vomited, and the one time he took me hiking, I fainted. My muscles ache already, but I fight the urge to stop.

His breathing is steady as he passes me. My breathing sounds like my body has forgotten what normal lungs are meant to sound like. I suck in air, gulping it down like water. He turns and begins to run backwards, his hands resting against his chest. He smiles as he watches me.

I try one final burst to catch him off guard. I hold the lead for three seconds. Then four. Then five. I continue to push my legs, fearing that one will not move as fast as the other and I will smash to the ground. But they keep moving. As I suck down the cool air, it stings my windpipe and my lungs burn. Behind me I can hear him coughing. I slow down, trying not to trip over my feet in the process. When I turn around he is metres behind me. He's stopped running.

*

We sit around my sister Sophie's dining table. Everyone is leaning back, in full food coma mode, Sophie's friends chatting among themselves. Sophie is picking at her plate while her boyfriend's arm drapes lazily over the back of her chair. Theo sits beside me, lounging a little and enjoying his full belly. 'I'm just going to the bathroom,' I whisper into his ear as I give his shoulder a quick squeeze.

Sophie doesn't lose a second. She pounces. 'I'll help,' she says, standing up across the table. I smirk at her.

'You're going to help me go to the bathroom?'

'Yes,' Sophie says, moving around her chair before I can stop her.

I look back at Theo, who's staring at me with eyes that beg, 'please don't be long'. He's done so well tonight, making conversation and responding to Sophie's questions firing at him from across the table. I squeeze his shoulder one more time and head towards the hallway. Some couples nuzzle or kiss, but that's not our style. We squeeze. Just a small amount of pressure that reminds the other one, 'I'm here and it's okay'.

I reach the bathroom, but Sophie swoops in front of me and leans herself against the door before I can open it. This has always been her signature move. Sure she's small, but no one ever pushes Sophie out of the way when she does the infamous swoop.

'I like him,' Sophie announces to me.

'That's great,' I tell her. I keep my face deadpan, but my heart flutters.

'He's really wonderful, El. Easily one of the best you've brought 'round.'

'I want to use the toilet,' I say. She's still standing there, a smirk playing across her face. We'll be here until she decides we are done.

'Did you have to ask him so many questions?' I ask.

'I wanted to get to know him,' she says.

'Yes. But you also wanted to know how much he would let you ask. It was a test,' I retort.

'And he passed with flying colours. Didn't run out of the room or even assess his closest exits. He's open and funny and kind. You should marry him now,' Sophie chuckles.

'Oh calm down. We're not even serious yet. He hasn't met Mum.'

'Come on, El, he's obviously into you. He's spent all his time chatting to everyone and looks at you so adoringly. It's real for him.'

'I don't know if it's real for me, though,' I say.

Sophie looks at me knowingly, her lips a little pouted. Her raised eyebrows say it all. She doesn't believe a bar of it.

'Can I bloody pee now?' My bladder pulses. Maybe I'll be the first person to push my sister out of the way after all.

Sophie finally opens the door and lets me through.

'You know I'm right!' I hear her calling down the

hall as I close the door and lock it.

When I arrive back at the table, I see Sophie has plonked herself down in my chair, right next to Theo.

'Well, what did I miss?' I casually ask the group.

I glance at Theo and his eyes don't plead back. He's comfortable sitting with Sophie. Seeing him so relaxed, warmth wells deep inside my chest. Damn it, I smile to myself.

*

A speaker crackles, followed by 'Good evening and welcome to the NGV's Vincent van Gogh exhibit. We are just letting the previous session finish up and will let you in shortly.'

I stare at the stained-glass ceiling above me. The colours glisten, the moon and the city outside illuminating the panels. Theo stands next to me, explaining the architecture of the ceiling, the room, the whole building. 'The stained glass was created by Leonard French. He was actually born in Brunswick. Pretty cool, huh? He's got some panels in the National Library of Australia as well.' He coughs, though I'm not sure if it's genuine or to get my attention. 'And just look at the exposed masonry. It's the oldest gallery in Australia,' he says. My eyes flick from one stained-glass panel to the next, soaking in the kaleidoscope of colours.

I bounce on the balls of my feet to keep myself warm. Each time the door opens, a fresh gust of winter wind sweeps through. The city rushes past, cars and trams streaming along St Kilda Road.

Theo coughs again, one small cough. Then another. And another. Each cough bigger than the last. He forces his face into his elbow. People turn to stare and I smile apologetically. They smile back politely. I do my best to shuffle him away slightly while keeping our place in the queue.

I rub his back. My cheeks feel hot. People keep staring. They watch me, waiting for me to do more, to pull out an inhaler, to start CPR; who knows what they want from me. I wait, continue to pat his back, anger boiling in my stomach.

The coughs get harder and heavier until he is panting to catch his breath. People start shuffling away from us. A staff member walks over with a bottle of water. I accept it and thank them before forcing Theo to drink a mouthful. He struggles with the first sip, then swallows the next few gulps easily. The coughing eases into jagged breaths. I should wait, let him catch his breath. But I don't.

'Have you gone to the doctor yet?' He gives a small nod as he takes another few mouthfuls.

'Are you on antibiotics? It's driving me insane.'

'No antibiotics. Doctor's running tests.' He pulls a tissue from his pocket and wipes it across his mouth, cleaning up the spit.

'What tests?' My stomach is a knot. His face softens, and he moves closer to me. I can feel how warm he is through the sleeves of his sweater.

'Blood tests. They're looking for infection.'

'Well it's clearly in there.' I poke at his chest.

'El, they think it's something else.'

'What?'

He takes my hands in his. They're soft and warm as they wrap around my own. His eyes look solemn. He doesn't blink.

'Bub. They don't know.'

The doors slide open and closed again and another swoop of wind rushes in. I breathe it in and feel it pierce my throat and sit heavily in my chest. I slide my arms under his and wrap myself around him, nuzzling my face into his chest. He holds me and gently rocks us side to side, his cheek pressed to the top of my head. We stand like this for as long as we can. I don't want to know what's wrong. I never want to let go.

Theo pulls away from me slowly and kisses my forehead. He slips his fingers between mine and we move forward in the line. People are looking at us. We have made quite the scene. We drift into the gallery, Theo pulling me slowly along. The first painting we see is of a lone figure surrounded by trees.

Part II

Theo

She's a few steps ahead of me, like she almost always is: in study, in work, in life and, despite her significantly shorter legs, in distance along the scuffed concrete path. She's dancing, her skirt blowing up in the cold Melbourne wind. She catches the silky black fabric and swishes it back down towards her feet, sending it swinging to the other side of her legs. She half turns and looks at me over her shoulder. Her hair falls slightly across her face and the city lights catch the streaks of blue in her eyes. My heart feels like it's punching its way through my chest. Or is it trying to heave its way up my throat? It is too full of love. She is beautiful. She rolls her eyes and turns back. I walk faster and fall into step beside her.

'That was amazing,' she says, still humming to herself. 'Did you like it?'

'I did. More than I expected. Bloody catchy songs.'

'Well, I loved it.' She drops her skirt and scoops up my hand. I love the way her fingers feel in mine. 'Can we go to other musicals? It could be our special date night. I want to see *Aladdin* and *Wicked* and *Moulin Rouge* and *Hamilton* …' She trails off, but I know she's still listing them in her head. There's a skip in her step.

I kiss her hand. 'Of course.'

'Promise?' She stops in the middle of the path and holds out her pinky. People flow around us on Spring Street. Taxis rush down Little Bourke and people crowd the pedestrian crossing to Parliament Station. The city moves, but she stands still.

We both know her pinky promises are silly, but I also know they mean something to her. A physical seal, I think they make her feel safe and understood and heard. 'I promise,' I say, taking her pinky in mine and shaking it a little to make her laugh.

Months later, we will see an ad for *Aladdin*. Neither of us will say anything. But we will both know that I broke our promise.

*

Racing Ella home from the station is normally fun, but right now I feel like my lungs are about to explode.

'What'd you do, swallow a fly?' she calls, walking back to me in that ridiculous but cute sports outfit. 'Maybe you aren't as fit as you thought,' she teases.

I bend over, my hands resting on my knees as I cough, spluttering onto the nature strip. My backpack is discarded on the grass. Gobs of spit dangle from my mouth. Each cough is excruciating.

'Shit!' Her eyes widen as she races back to me. She helps me to sit on the grass. The coughing has eased, but breathing is still hard. My shoulders heave with every breath and I cough each time my lungs expand as though there is something pressing back against them. I push my hands against the centre of my chest, massaging it gently. Digging through my backpack, Ella pulls out a handful of tissues and passes them to me to wipe my mouth. When I'm done, she holds out her hand to take the tissues back. Her hands shake as she scrunches the used tissues into a little ball in her fist and walks them over to the nearest bin along the sidewalk. She returns, squats next to me and rubs her hand across my back.

'Theo, what happened?'

'I've just got a bit of a cough,' I wheeze, trying to force a smile.

My breathing steadies into light, shallow breaths and I straighten my back. I cough again and my shoulders fall forward. I keep my shoulders tucked and continue massaging my chest with my palm.

'That's not just a cough. It sounds as if you're hacking up a lung. You can run twice that distance without breaking a sweat. What the hell?'

'I've been a bit under the weather. I'll be on antibiotics soon and back to racing your butt in no time.' She looks at me, concerned, and leans against me. I wrap my arms around her. She nuzzles her face against my chest.

'You stress too much,' I say. 'But how about we just walk the rest of the way home.' I pick up my backpack and swing it over my shoulder. Then I lift her hand and kiss it. We walk back to the house, our fingers locked. The streetlights flicker above our heads. The wind has dropped off, leaving the streets quiet and empty. Scattered leaves on the road crunch beneath our feet.

*

'What'll you do when you finish uni?' I ask Ella.

She closes her eyes while she thinks. Her eyelashes look so soft against her skin; I just want to trace my fingers across her cheeks. I slip my fingers through hers, playing with her hand instead. I could stay here forever, stretched out on this bed listening to her. She asks me what I want to do. I list them all off, the things I want to see, to smell, to eat.

Then I blurt out, 'Do you want to come with me?'

'Want to come with you where?' She hasn't understood. I should just stop now. But my mouth is already moving.

'To London.'

'You want me to come live with you? In London?' She doesn't scoff. She just sounds curious.

'Well, yeah, why not?' Why not? Why not?! I scream inside my head. Well, maybe because you haven't lived together in your own country, you psycho. Or that you haven't travelled together further than a few hours to Daylesford. Or maybe because people actually consider these types of questions before just blurting them out in a normal conversation.

I wonder if I've always come on too strong. Maybe I have exes out there who tell stories about the stage-five clinger they once dated. Maybe Ella will tell stories about the stage-five clinger who invited her to live in London with him after they had been together for all of five minutes. I wouldn't blame her. I would probably even laugh about it if I heard it myself, under different circumstances obviously. Should I try digging myself out of the hole or just curl up and hide in it? Best get your shovel, Theo.

'Fuck. It's too soon to ask that. Way too soon. Fuck's sake. Sorry. Forget it, forget I said anything. Too much pressure. Sorry.' My mouth feels loose and numb. Words pour out like water. I may as well be holding a big sign that reads 'Don't leave me!' Pathetic. Dig up, dig up!

My heart is raging against my chest. She hasn't said anything. She must think I'm crazy, must be figuring out how to let me down gently and get me out of her house. Why the hell did I say that?

Then she's laughing. Hard. Laughing at me? Fuck, please, please don't let her be laughing at me.

'You probably think I'm crazy now,' I say.

She squeezes my hand and says, 'I would love to live in London with you.' I'm so prepared for her to have said 'no' that it takes my brain a minute to process. I feel my muscles stretch in delight as my face breaks into a smile. We'll conquer you one day, London!

*

We stand at the front gate to her sister's apartment block, its windows looming above. I feel Ella's hand slip into my coat pocket, her fingers twisting between mine. She gives a quick squeeze. I rub my thumb across hers and she smiles up at me. I should've told her. I should have fucking told her.

'Ready to go in?' Her hand pulls me forward.

No, I'm not ready to go in. I can't do this. My blood pumps faster, my chest feels like it might burst. Am I having a heart attack? I start counting my heartbeats. I imagine the blood pushing its way out of the tiny hole in my elbow crease, leaking through the bandage and seeping out over her sister's dining table. Deep breaths. The cold air burns as I draw it in. I choke down the lump in my throat.

'Alright, yep. Let's go.' Is my voice usually this high? Maybe she can't tell. You'd think I'd be prepared for this. It's just meeting her sister for godsakes.

She's looking at me.

I can't tell her now. Why didn't I tell her before?

'It's gonna be great,' she says. She stretches up and kisses my cheek.

I step forward, half because if I don't move now I won't move at all and half because she's pulling me along. The wine bottle clangs against the metal gate as I push it open. Don't drop the wine, don't drop the wine, don't drop the wine. She readjusts the bouquet of flowers I insisted on bringing. I should've brought a smaller bunch. I didn't want them to look shit, but now I think they're too big. I've fucked it already and we haven't even made it inside.

We climb the flight of stairs in silence. I walk behind her, trying to keep my breaths even. Force down the cough. Hold it in. Swallow the lump. Ella navigates us through the hallways. Fuck. I wasn't watching. I'll never find my way back if I need to leave. Not that I can leave anyway. Too late to tell her and too late to not be here.

She lets herself in without knocking, puts the flowers down on the kitchen counter, then rushes over to the sink where a woman is rinsing lettuce leaves – Sophie. Sophie drops the strainer and gives her sister a clumsy, wet-handed hug.

My fingers are wrapped around the neck of the wine bottle like a chokehold. I feel its weight trying to slip through my hand. I grip it harder. Don't drop the wine, don't drop the wine, don't drop the wine. Did Ella say Sophie drank red or white? Or was it meant to be sparkling?

Sophie releases Ella and turns to me. I smile at her. Is it a good smile?

'You must be Theo,' she says.

I offer up my right hand. Sophie sweeps past it and scoops me into a hug, restraining my arms and pressing on the bruise on my elbow. I lift my free arm and pat her back awkwardly. I look around for Ella to save me. She looks so happy to see Sophie and me in the same room. I've got to make this work.

'Let me take your coats!' Sophie beams. Ella has already taken hers off and tossed it over the back of a chair. They both look at me. I don't move. I can't take the coat off without showing Sophie the bandage. She might ask questions. What if she guesses? I don't know if I can hold it together if she does. Could I lie to both of them or would my face give me away this time? My mind races with what I have and haven't told Ella. What if I slip up, tell her too much or get my words wrong? Ella has already seen the bandage, but I don't want to remind her of its existence. I should've told her. I should've told her and let her come to her sister for comfort. Why didn't I wear a long-sleeve shirt? Why are they looking at me? Fuck.

'It's fine, thank you.' Fuck. 'I'll keep mine on.' Ella's eyes narrow at me.

'Babe, take your coat off.' Fuck-fuck-fuck. 'You'll get hot.' I won't take it off.

'Nah, I'd like to keep it on,' I say with more force. I rub my hand up and down my arm to warm myself. I even do a fake shiver. Why did I do that? Ella watches.

'Theo, take your coat off.'

'El, it's fine,' Sophie says. 'He can leave it on if he wants.'

I should've told her.

We all sit at the dining table. Sophie and her boyfriend, Ella and me, and some of their old friends from school. I'm not ready for this. My legs jostle under the table. Ella rests her hand on my knee, her silent way of telling me to stop. I try, but I can barely control it. I feel like I'm going to be sick or cough up a lung, or spit the little lump right out onto the table. Push it down, Theo, push it down.

Sophie offers the wine bottle around the table. 'Theo, you've barely touched yours,' she says. Shit.

What do I say? Sorry, Soph, I can't drink that delicious wine, my doctors have asked me to abstain from any unnecessary toxins right now? Obviously not going with that line. Think quick, think quick.

'It was a gift for you. I shouldn't be drinking it.' Yeah, totally nailed it, Theo, good one. If I could roll my eyes at myself, I would.

'Oh, don't bother about that,' she says, dribbling more wine into my still-full glass. They all stare at me. Oh my god, why won't they look away? I lift the glass and take a sip. They keep watching me. I take another sip. The wine catches in my throat. I try to swallow, but it splutters back up. I feel it dribble out of my mouth and down my chin. And then I'm coughing. Fuck's sake. I need to get control of it. Hold it in. I press my tongue against the roof of my mouth. But it doesn't work. The coughs burst out. I spit wine and saliva all over Sophie's dinner. I cover my face with my hands, as much for the cough as for the shame. I need to get the fuck out of here. My throat sears as if a burning rod has been shoved down it. Ella rubs her hand across my back.

'Are you okay?' she asks.

I can't reply, but even if I could, I wouldn't. Why did I come? Ella would've had just as good a time without me, probably better after this fiasco. I should've known I wouldn't keep it together. What a fucking mess.

Sophie brings over a glass of water and I gulp it

down. It takes another two glasses to get the coughing to ease, but the heavy lump still sits in my chest.

'Wrong pipe,' I explain, pointing at my throat. My voice is raspy, like a pack-a-day smoker. Everyone nods and smiles politely.

*

We have the house to ourselves. My parents have gone out so I can do this in private. Ella arrived just after they left, missing them by minutes. One less pressure to deal with. I wish it were different. I hope she won't be mad, but I'm sure she'll be disappointed.

It's strange having her sit on my parents' couch for the first time. I thought I could make it normal – her sitting here reading her book, me playing games on the PlayStation to calm myself down. I breathe in and out in time with the buttons. Now or never, buddy. I wish I could choose never.

'Hey El?'

'Mm-hmm?'

What do I say … make conversation first or just jump right in? Is there a right way to say this? Probably. Whatever it is, they don't tell you that in the leaflets.

Fuck. I don't want to tell her. Once I tell her there'll be a before and an after.

I'll always be *that* guy she dated.

Just spit it out. I hold down the bile I feel building in my stomach. I'm still pressing the controller, the rhythm keeping me breathing. In, *clack-clack-clack*. Out, *clack-clack-clack*. I should take my eyes off the screen, but I can't. I can't look at her. She knows it's coming. I don't want to tell her. I want to choke it down with the coughs. The quiet is tense between us. She is waiting.

I say the words. They linger in the room, hanging limply in the silent air. It doesn't feel better to say it. I don't feel like a weight has been lifted by telling her. Instead, it all presses down on me, heavier than ever before.

She's trying to hold her face still. Tears start trickling down her cheeks. I pull her towards me and she shifts easily into my arms, resting her head on my chest. I can feel the tears seep through my shirt.

Her head is just above the nine-centimetre tumour sitting above my lung.

Part III

Ella

The PlayStation controller clicks as Theo slams his fingers against the buttons. *Clack-clack-clack.* He presses them over and over. I can't discern the pattern but I'm sure it's there. *Clack-clack-clack.* The players run across the screen, Theo's body following their movements. Sometimes he talks to them like a coach, not realising he's saying things out loud. But not today. Today he grunts when he makes a mistake and breathes out when a play works.

I've been reading the same page of my book for the last ten minutes.

'Hey El?'

'Mm-hmm?'

Clack-clack-clack.

'Yeah?' I say, folding the corner of my page. He's not looking at me.

Clack-clack-clack.

I keep watching him. His eyes dart across to look at me and then dart back to the screen just as quickly.

'What?' I nudge him.

Clack-clack-clack.

'You know how I was having those tests.'

I can't tell if it's a question or a statement. 'Yeah?'

His eyes are still staring at the screen and his fingers rest on the controller. His lips are pressed together like he's holding in a bad taste. He finally looks at me.

'It's cancer.'

Hodgkin's lymphoma, he tells me. I can see it pains him to say it. He didn't want to tell me. He would've undisclosed it rather than upset me and buried all the pain deep inside himself. I try to keep my face still, but I can already feel the sobs catch in my throat. I try to stop them. I don't want to make this harder for him. I have to be stoic, supportive, strong. This is not about me. But tears slide down my cheeks no matter how much I will them not to. He sets the controller aside and wraps himself around me. I lean on his chest, his sweater scratching against my cheek, and listen to his heart.

*

Our bodies tangle together under the sheets. His smell mixes with mine, a warm, close smell. I slip my arms around his body and trace my fingers across his back. I feel each mole, each chickenpox scar, each part of his body that has become as familiar to me as my own. I soak it in, the pressure of his lips against mine. Though I don't mean it to, my mind starts to wander. What if this is our last time? What if he goes into hospital and never comes out? It's a small chance, but it's one that has firmly lodged itself in my mind.

Small groans slip from his mouth. He bends his head down closer to mine. 'I love you,' he whispers in my ear.

The tears leak out before I even know they are coming. They drip off my face and onto the sheets beneath me. I can't stem the flow. I sweep my hand across my face and it comes away wet. Our bodies continue to move together. I hold his head gently, feeling his warm breath against my neck.

'I love you too,' I whisper back. My voice breaks.

'El, are you crying?' he asks. He slows his movements and rests his hand against my cheek.

'Yeah,' I whisper back. I press my head into his hand and let him kiss my forehead. 'I'm gonna miss this.' He knows I mean more than the sex.

'I'm so sorry,' he whispers. He cradles me in his arms and rocks me like a child.

*

'You don't have to stick around for this,' he says. His fingers are shaking – from nerves or from skipping his morning coffee, I can't tell.

'I don't mind,' I tell him. 'I have the day off anyway.' I don't tell him that I've taken the day off to be here for another doctor's appointment. I don't want him to know that I'm missing work for this, like he told me not to. I grab his hands and hold them. His fingers are still shaking but slow a little as I run my thumb across the inside of his half-clenched palm.

'I don't mean that you don't have to be *here*,' he says, slipping his fingers out from mine and moving my hand into my lap. 'I don't mean today. I mean, at all. For any of it.' He looks around the waiting room, his body turns slightly away from mine.

I lean forward, trying to catch his eye. 'I don't

understand,' I say. I drove us here. I'm his ride home. Then I feel it. The headache pressing, lightly at first, against the back of my skull. Sleep deprivation, the doctor told me. The body reacting to stress. Need to get eight hours of sleep a night. Most nights I sleep for three and stare at the ceiling for the other five.

Theo takes a deep breath and starts bouncing his legs up and down. I give up trying to catch his eye and look instead at the other patients. An older lady sits with her knees together, ankles crossed, reading a battered copy of *Women's Weekly*. Another couple sits a few seats away. The woman looks pale. She's wearing a knitted beanie. Where golden curls or a brown bob might have stuck out the bottom, there is nothing. I can suddenly feel my own hair. Thousands of strands and the ends poking against my neck. I should've worn it pulled back, bunched it all together and hidden it, pushed behind my ears at least. I move to sweep it back into a tight ponytail, but I lose courage and reach out to Theo instead. I put my hand between his shoulders. His body starts to relax into me, but then his face tightens and he leans away.

I drop my hand and look back at the couple. The woman's shirt hangs loose and empty around her chest. The man's clothes fit snugly, causing little bulges under his sweater. They look like a set. She is thin and shallow; he is wide and dense. Both have bags under their eyes and the same whitish skin that's seen more fluorescent light than sun.

Were they like us? How long had they been together before the illness entered their lives? Were they in their twenties or their thirties when it arrived? Their current age is impossible to tell. I see them sitting in a pub sharing jugs of beer with friends. Her hair flowing down her back and her laugh ringing out through the bar.

How many times has he sat in the adjacent room while she dry-retched? How long did he hold her hair back before it fell out and there was nothing left to hold? I imagine them wandering the lemur enclosure at Melbourne Zoo, posing for photos and pulling faces for the camera. He smiles and probably thinks he's the luckiest man to have found her.

How much longer do they have? Do they know their time line, or is every day an equal mix of hope, desperation and fear? I see them dancing together on the balcony while curry simmers in the kitchen. Their bodies move to the evening sounds of the suburbs, the clatter of next door's plates, the rustle of birds settling into their nests for the night.

Look at us here. Us and them. How long have they got? How long have *we* got? They look back at me sympathetically and smile.

Theo tilts himself towards me and I'm pulled back to the present. 'I mean you don't have to do this,' he says and waves around the room. 'Any of this.' He's still not fully looking at me. 'You don't have to stay with me.' The words spill out of him and land at my feet. Then: silence, and the sound of the waiting-room clock. I want to scoop up his sentences and push them into my bag, into a pocket, tuck them away somewhere private where no one can hear them. The pressure in my head is building, expanding into every nook in my brain and pounding at my temples. I want to scream. I want to slam this chair through the window.

'What are you saying, Theo?'

His legs keep jiggling. I want to reach out and hold him still, press him down into the floor. He looks at me out of the corner of his eye, just a flicker, before turning away again. 'I don't want you to feel trapped,' he says.

I am trapped.

I leave now and I'm the girl who left when he got sick – the girl who abandoned her cancerous boyfriend. I stay and who knows what will happen.

Parallel universes spring up behind my eyes. The two of us sitting in another waiting room, weeks from now, having this conversation again. Sitting at a cafe, years from now, a few scars worse for wear, but still breathing. Sitting at different cafes, alone, wondering or not wondering about the other. Standing at the edge of Theo's grave, tossing a handful of sand on top of his coffin. Theo and I sitting in a hospital room ten, twenty, thirty years from now, our faces lined and our bodies worn. It's the last one I fear the most.

I want to leave. Does he know? I want to run from

this room and not come back. I want to have already left, got out early. I would be sitting at home, maybe still swiping through Tinder. Would that be better or worse? I won't leave — will I? I want to go back to before. Before Theo or before cancer? Some days I can't tell. I hate myself for even considering.

'Are you breaking up with me?' My face burns. The other patients pretend they aren't listening, but I know they are. I would listen. I would store it all up, collecting it like treasure to lay out for Theo later. You'll never guess what I heard in a waiting room today, I'd say. Yep, tried to dump her then and there. Can't believe it. Wonder if she considered it. Selfish bitch.

'I'm not breaking up with you,' he says. His tone is weary and tense. He enunciates each word like he doesn't have the time or the patience to explain it to me again. 'I'm just saying, if you don't want to be here then don't be. I'm giving you a guilt-free pass. The girl with the guy she couldn't dump because he got cancer …'

'It's not like that,' I say. But it *is* like that. Not always, but sometimes, enough to crawl under my skin and settle there. I can feel it coming — the starting to cry. I'm sick to death of crying in waiting rooms. My hands curl into fists. I want to smash them against him. I want to hit until one of us bleeds. I want to curl up and cry into his shoulder. 'This isn't fair, Theo. It's already hard, please don't make it harder.' I should've known he would try and do this. He probably thinks he's being noble, throwing himself on the sword to spare me. But all it does is hurt us both.

'You think I don't know it's not fair?' His shoulders hunch forward. He's still not looking at me. Why won't he look at me? His hair sweeps down across his forehead, the curls tangle in his eyelashes. He bats them away, wiping his eyes at the same time. 'I'm trying to make it fair. I'm trying to make it easier on you. Can't you see? I'm letting you out of it!'

The pain seeps behind my eyelids. I'm dizzy. Count to ten. My vision is blurry. One. Please don't faint. Two. Breathe, deep breaths, choke down the vomit. Three. Bile burns in my throat.

'This shit's about to get really fucked up,' he says, still keeping his voice even. 'And if you're going to bail halfway through, I'd rather you do it now.' His voice quavers on the last few words.

All rational thought is gone. I am stung by his words. 'Where is this coming from? What reason have I given you to throw this at me? Are you doing this to protect me or do you really think I'm going to abandon you?' I'm spitting the whispers at him. The old lady has put her magazine down. She stares at the painting as she listens to our conversation. I look at the other couple again. How many times have they had this conversation? He never left her. I read in his eyes that he won't leave her. Jealousy stings in my chest. I hate this stranger for his certainty, his loyalty, his love. I look at Theo. 'This is hard enough without you trying to push me away.'

'I'm trying to do the right thing here.' His voice cracks. He runs his hands through his hair and pulls the strands back, the skin becoming taut across his forehead.

'Theodore,' the nurse calls. He stands and walks away, leaving me sitting in the waiting room.

My stomach releases and my fists unclench. I stop holding my breath and ease back in my seat, grateful for the moment alone. I want to lie down and sleep.

*

I'm in shock when Theo tells me. The treatment might not affect his sperm, or it might cause complete infertility. There is no way of knowing until it's done.

We have five years to use the sperm Theo has frozen before its quality begins to decline. In ten years it will no longer be usable. We lose one year to treatment and then another year to recovery. That leaves us still in our twenties with a handful of years left to decide. Who knows how much time it will take to get our lives back? Maybe there will be less time on the clock than we think.

I thought I didn't want kids. I still think I don't. But I always wanted the choice. 'You'll change your mind,' older women have always said to me. They repeat it like a mantra. I'm still not convinced I will, but I wanted that decision to be mine, not made for me by science and numbers.

And what about Theo. What if I'm taking these years from him? The clock ticks and our time runs down.

*

I stand out the front of St Vincent's Hospital. It's July in Melbourne and the wind is swirling through the street. I'm early. I need to give a good impression: the girlfriend who is on time, supportive, there when you need her. I don't know what his parents already know about me. Theo keeps everything so compartmentalised that I don't know much about them, so I imagine it is likely the same in return.

Cigarette smoke carries in the air. I'm always shocked by people smoking outside hospitals. It must feel like cheating death. Are they living on limited time anyway or are they beyond caring? I understand the terminal patients, but I can barely hide my gobsmacked expression when I see a smoking doctor or nurse. I turn away from the smokers, shielding myself with my coat to try and block out the smell.

Theo is walking in-between his parents. They flank him like bodyguards. When they reach me, Theo leans in and gives me a kiss. I kiss him back, but it feels weird in front of his parents. I'm not good with PDA at the best of times.

'Mum, Dad, this is Ella,' Theo says. 'Ella, this is my mum, Tina, and my dad, Robert.'

Robert stretches out his hand to shake mine. His grip is firm but gentle. Tina pulls me into a warm, friendly hug.

'Hi,' I say. 'So good to meet you both.'

'Lovely to meet you,' Tina says. 'Finally. Theo's been hiding you away. Did he invite you to Easter? Or Yiayia's birthday dinner?'

My blank expression answers her questions. She turns on Theo. He is easily a head taller than her, but he still slumps slightly under her gaze. 'You didn't invite her? I told you to invite her.' She redirects her gaze back to me. 'I'm sorry, love. It's a shame. We wanted to meet you sooner.'

I know they've wanted to meet me for some time. My heart beats fast and my thumb rubs quickly across my palm, wiping away little balls of old skin.

'Mum. I wasn't going to invite her to something where she had to meet the whole family. Sometimes people don't like to meet thirty new people at a time. Especially if those people are your boyfriend's family.'

'Theo, don't exaggerate. It wouldn't have been the *whole* family.'

'Mum, some people need a little more time to settle into a relationship.' Theo's voice is gentle. He has been balancing us all – my desire to take things slow and his parent's desire to know who I am.

Robert says nothing. Instead, he looks calm and thoughtful, watching me and Theo. He and Theo share a lot of similarities, with the same long nose and brown eyes. If I ever wondered what Theo would look like in his sixties, Robert is probably a pretty accurate image.

'Oh well, looks like we're going to have lots of time to get to know each other,' Tina says. I can't tell if she's saying these things for me or for Theo, who's trying to look like it doesn't bother him. His hand finds mine and grips my fingers tightly.

'Should we go in and get this thing started then?' Theo says and waves at the door. Even in this situation, he has flair. I admire him for it. The rest of us nod because he's the one who has to be ready for this. Hand in hand, we walk in first. I look back at his parents and they both smile as they follow us in.

*

'I called the agent.'

'And?' he asks.

'It's all fine. They'll put the house back up for lease. They won't charge us because of our "exceptional circumstances". I didn't tell them that "exceptional" was a poor choice of word.'

We flop down onto his bed. The one he has slept in through primary school and high school and will now continue to sleep in. I close my eyes.

'Are you okay?' he asks. I can feel his breath. He is leaning over me, examining my face, trying to read it. I make it unreadable.

'I'm fine.'

'Bub, come on. Talk to me.'

I open my eyes and there he is. 'I'm just disappointed,' I say. 'I know there is nothing we can do about it, but I'm still upset. I wanted to live with you.'

'I wanted to live with you too.'

It had taken months to convince him to move out. I wonder how long it'll take next time.

'It just makes more sense to live at home,' Theo says. 'I don't want to burden you more than I already have.'

'But you're not a burden.'

'Not now,' he says.

*

He used to smell like laundry powder. Even with cologne, you could smell him underneath. Always the same smell. I would nuzzle my face into his chest and breathe it in. They didn't tell me his smell would change.

He doesn't smell like hospital, which I might've expected. Or the antibacterial products they spray and wash and wipe around him every day, a smell that soaks into your clothes and follows you well beyond the hospital. He doesn't smell like the mouthwash either, used three times a day to prevent ulcers and poor gum health from his chemical-laced saliva.

He smells like poison. It's a sickly sweet, noxious smell that mixes with his sweat. It seeps through his clothes and his sheets and lingers on his skin. He smells cold and unwelcoming, like meat gone off. I know he scratches at himself in the shower, trying to scrape the smell off. It doesn't work. It's in him now, as much part of him as the lump in his chest.

*

'Honey, can I get you anything?' Tina asks Theo. This is the fifth time this hour. She will move around the room, fluffing his pillows when he's too tired to sit up and shift his food tray to different places around the room even though he's too nauseous to eat.

Chemo sessions are like funerals. The family are there just as much for themselves as for Theo. We need to be there and watch it happen – to make it feel like we are helping. Like maybe there is something we can do for him, no matter how small. It is excruciating. But it's all worth it when you can help him to the toilet or run to the shops for comfier pants or the potato chips he's craving. There aren't many ways for us to help, but the smallest duty gives us comfort. It's because of this that I don't often begrudge Tina and her nurturing.

'Ella, can you get me another blanket?' Theo asks.

'Yeah, of course.' I go to stand, but before I can even straighten my legs Tina is waving for me to sit back down.

'Don't worry, I'll get it,' she says. I know she means well, but I'm frustrated all the same. I drop back into the chair, making sure it squeaks when I land. Robert looks at me and raises an eyebrow. It's the same look Theo would've given me had he been paying attention. I cross my arms and watch Tina walk out to the nurses' station. She comes back in with two blankets and an extra pillow, folds them across gently and slips the pillow down beside him. She settles herself back into her chair.

'Can you get me more water?' he asks me. The water jug sits on the tray table between him and me, just out of his reach. I stretch out my arm.

'I've got it,' Tina says and hops back up.

'Tina, stop.' My tone is sharp. I'm standing now, trying to soften it. 'I can help too. Let me help.' I pour Theo a glass of water and sit on his bed while he takes the few gulps to empty it.

'Thank you,' he says. His eyes are drooping the way they do when he's fighting to stay awake.

'It's okay. Go to sleep,' I tell him. His breathing steadily turns into deep inhalations and then snores. Tina and I both watch him sleep. I can feel her eyes shift to me, watching me watching him.

'I'm sorry, Ella. I just want to do what I can for him,' she says.

'I know. I do too.'

*

Compared with the hospital room, the house is peaceful. The light bounces off the hardwood floors. It's a nice change to the white vinyl of St Vincent's. The quiet simmer of pasta instead of the beep of the heart rate monitor or the *tick-tick-tick* of the chemicals pumping into his veins. The comfortable silence between us rather than the tense chats with family and friends, many of whom I meet for the first time in the hospital room. It's nice to be alone together. We have so few moments alone. The daylight hours are shared with his mum and dad and sometimes his sister, squished together in the small room. The night-time hours are filled with friends and nurses.

I lift a glass of lemonade to my lips and feel the tiny bursts of fizz hit my nose. I would love a glass of wine, but Theo isn't meant to drink, so lemonade it is.

'Theo, the pasta is starting to boil over,' I point out.

Theo glances over at it and then back to the sauce, still stirring away. 'Nah, it'll be fine.'

The lid of the pot begins shaking, its rattling growing more aggressive as the bubbles explode against it. Water drops start shooting out of the gaps like wet fireworks and small streams flow over the side and sizzle in the flames below.

'Theo, it's boiling too much. Just lower the heat and it'll stop,' I say.

Theo doesn't move or respond. The lid continues to clatter against the edge and the stream gets bigger. Water pools in the corners of the stovetop and drenches the white metal. I rush over and turn down the heat. The lid stops shaking and the water simmers down gently, the bubbles popping smaller and more infrequently through the swirling spaghetti.

Theo looks at the pot, as if noticing it for the first time. 'Sorry bub, I wasn't with it for a minute there,' he says, shaking his head to bring himself back.

'It's fine. But you better clean that when we're finished!' I tease.

'But I'm doing most of the cooking,' Theo gestures at the stovetop.

'But I'm the one who stopped it from bubbling over completely. I saved your butt. You could've been cleaning up a much worse mess.'

'Shit! The garlic bread,' Theo winces.

Theo tentatively pulls out a charred brick that used to be garlic bread. He drops it into the sink and steam rises up around it. His shoulders slump as he stares at the black lump.

The smoke alarm screams through the house. I grab the tea towel from where it was last tossed on the bench and whip it above my head, waving it like a white flag of surrender. The smoke swirls through the air, curling around the fabric and the alarm. I slow my waving as the alarm settles itself into silence.

I move around the bench and throw open the kitchen window, letting the cool evening air sweep into the room. The breeze disperses the smoke, tendrils weaving their way up and out into the night.

'I'm sorry this is all going so shit,' Theo says.

I wrap my arms around his waist and rest my head against his back. We stand like this for a second, enjoying the stillness.

I unravel myself from him and lift the lid off the steaming pot. The smell wafts out and fills the kitchen

– a rich, warming smell. I take a fork, twist a string of spaghetti around it, dip it in the red sauce and pop it into my mouth. 'Theo, it's actually really good.'

He ruffles his hand through his hair. That's his tell – he's embarrassed. As his hand comes away from his head, so does a chunk of hair. It peels away easily from his scalp and slips through his fingers, floating down through the air and landing in the middle of the pot. Stray hairs drift around him and fall onto the stovetop and the bench next to him. The sauce bubbles and drowns the hairs into its red depths.

'I guess we're gonna see what kind of scalp I've got under here,' Theo says.

*

In the hospital at night we get the illusion of privacy. His family goes home for their nightly routine, eating dinner together, preparing for the next day, caring for Theo's aging yiayia. That's when I climb onto Theo's bed and delicately wrap the tubes around myself so I can curl up next to him. I lie still and cautious beside him, careful not to tug or pull or move anything. Sometimes I can feel the cold liquid move through the tube across my chest and into his arm.

The nurses knock and try to make their checks fast and discreet. But there's always a look on their faces, a look that says they have seen this before. The look reminds me we are in a hospital. It says, 'I pity you.' I know they're being sympathetic, but it still hurts. I pity us too.

*

I miss the sex. Not just the physical stuff, but the closeness. I miss the intimacy. We haven't kissed in months. And haven't had sex for longer. I would calculate it, but I know it would just upset me more. It feels like years.

We're technically allowed to have sex, but we have to be very careful. Not that we weren't already – neither of us wants kids, let alone in our twenties. But now it's more than sexual health and babies. Now, his sperm is 'dangerous'. I imagine it's fluoro green and burns like acid when it touches skin, melting away the flesh. Apparently, it's not quite as dramatic as that, but it's still not good to be around.

Even kissing has its dangers. No kissing at all during his treatment sessions because his saliva has remnants of the poison that runs through his body. Kissing also has the risk that I will make him sick, letting in loose germs that will wreak havoc on his suppressed immune system. Neither of us has said it, but I think we are both too scared to kiss anymore. I know I'm not willing to risk it.

This is the longest I've gone without sex in a relationship. I assume I won't be having sex for another few weeks or even months. It could be longer if the chemo hasn't worked. I can't imagine that. I know it's selfish. I know there are worse things. But my mind still dwells on it. I haven't talked to Theo about it. I can't. Then his mind would dwell on it too.

'Just do it yourself,' friends tell me. It's not the same.

I imagine being the girl who cheats on her cancer boyfriend. I can't.

*

'Do you want to go to the zoo?' I ask.

We lie on his bed. Theo stares at the ceiling. I stare at my computer screen hopelessly trying to write an essay. I need to get out of the house. We've got three days before Theo is back in hospital for another chemo round, which means we have three days of his immune system being strong enough to leave the house. Our last date was two months ago. We haven't been to the zoo since before he got sick.

'No,' he replies. 'Not meant to be around animals.'

'Or a cafe?'

'I can't drink coffee.' He rolls away from me, towards the wall. I set my laptop aside on the bed and curl myself around his body.

'You don't have to have coffee. You could have a hot chocolate? Or a muffin?'

'I'm already fat enough. I don't need to add anything more.'

I try to keep my voice light, but with two ideas so quickly shot down, I'm struggling to think of a third. I can't leave him, but I can't bear another day of lying around. The 'what ifs' start rolling through my mind. What if the chemo doesn't work and my last memories of us are months of lying around and sleeping? I just want something to hold onto, something that makes me feel like we're a normal couple again.

'Well, what about we just go for a walk? We could go to a park or just sit in the sun.'

'No,' he says. 'I don't want to do anything. Stop trying to make it better for me.'

It takes all my willpower not to shake him. He hasn't asked how I am in days. He doesn't ask how I'm coping anymore. Not many people do. I know it's selfish, but I can't help feeling like we were meant to be a team and now I'm the one struggling under the weight of both of us.

'I'm not trying to make it better for you.' My voice rises as I sit up. I remember his parents are downstairs, so I force myself to lower it. 'I'm trying to make it better for me. I'm stuck inside just as often as you are and I'm getting fucking sick of it. All I do is sit here and watch you lie in bed. We've got three whole days that you can go outside and you can't even get yourself out of bed for me? Fuck. Sometimes things have to be for me too, Theo. It's hard for me too.'

'I'm sorry,' he whispers, but he doesn't move.

*

My phone buzzes in my pocket. I ignore it and keep typing on my computer, wishing I could sleep on the library desk instead. The phone goes off again. It's accusing in its meekness, just like Theo; it whispers my guilt back to me. I know he never means to make me feel guilty, but I feel it anyway. My life doesn't stop because he's been forced to pause his. Some days I wish it would stop. I just need a minute to catch my breath.

I keep typing. My fingers feel tight, the knuckles aching. My computer keys are old and sound clackety as I press them.

My phone buzzes again. Without looking, I toss it into my handbag. It keeps buzzing. I ignore it. I want to be there. I want to be here. I just need time to myself. Just this one day for me to get my shit done. How does my world keep turning so fast while his stands so still?

There is a short moment of reprieve before my phone starts buzzing again. The vibration shakes the bag against my foot. This time, people turn to look at me. Between my phone and my clackety keys, I wouldn't want someone like me in the library either.

I give up, slamming the lid of my laptop shut. I won't get any more done today. The guilt gnaws at my stomach. I fish through my handbag and pull out my phone. Eight messages and two missed calls. No voicemails.

Where are you?
Are you coming in today?
I thought you'd be here by now.

Where are you? Are you on your way?

Fine. Don't reply. Don't bother coming in.

Babe, I'm sorry. I'm just really worried. Message me when you get these.

Can you bring me some ginger beer when you come in? The nausea is bad today. The nurses said it might help.

I really need you to come.

*

I lie in my bed and stare into the darkness. Trick myself into seeing shapes, shadows moving in the dimness. I close my eyes and breathe deeply, pushing my body down into the mattress. I try to feel each of my muscles, tensing them one by one before releasing them. Since Theo's diagnosis I've been seeing a counsellor, who suggests I practise mindfulness. But my mind is so full that I can't stop the thoughts from racing one another around my head like a dog chasing its tail.

Breathe. Feel your body. Be present in the moment. Feel your muscles. Think about now. Think about him. Think about him now. Think about if he's okay. Think about if he will be okay. Stop thinking about if he's going to be okay. Think about thinking about other things. Think about now.

I lift my phone and click the home button. The screen is too bright. No new notifications. He's probably asleep, but I try anyway.

Hey. Are you awake?
Send.
Wait.
Nothing.

I can't sleep.
Send.
Wait.
Nothing.

Breathe like they taught me. In for four. Hold for four. Out for four. I stare at the roof again. In. Hold. Out. I hear the wind whistling past the window outside. A tree branch scrapes against the glass panes, the leaves rustling like they want to come inside. In. Hold. Out.

I miss you.
Send.
Wait.

*

Theo is asleep. The blankets are twisted and lie across his torso. His stomach creeps out of his shirt, paunchy and hairless. I watch his chest rising and falling. The IV ticks as it drips saline into his vein. I step quietly across the room, careful not to squeak or bang or crash into anything.

I unpack my make-up onto the bathroom basin and poke and swipe and dab until my skin looks polished and not like I've spent the day in hospital. I've hidden the bags under my eyes. Hidden the oil in my hair. I'll hide the rest under teeth and lips that I'm hoping will turn into a real smile if I just pretend for long enough. I glance at my reflection in the mirror.

There. Normal. Almost.

I sneak back into the room and pull my shoes on. He's still asleep. I wiggle onto the bed and rest my head against the pillow. He rolls over and stretches his arm across my waist.

'El?'

'Mm-hmm?'

'Are you good?' He looks at me.

I smile at him. A real smile. 'Yeah, bub, I'm good.'

'Don't you have a party to get to?'

'Are you sure you're okay if I leave you?' I run my hand across his forehead. Is he warm? He feels hot. Maybe I should get a nurse? I don't remember when they last checked his temperature.

'I'm just gonna be lying here anyway. It's fine. Go. Have fun.' He tries to sit up, but he's too tired. His arm is still resting across my waist.

When did they check his blood pressure? Or his heart rate? Surely they are due back around soon. I move my fingers to his wrist and begin counting. I've never left before his final check during visiting hours. Normally the nurses are here by now. We know when they are running behind because of the way they move around the ward, but today has been calm. They should be here soon. I'll wait just a little longer.

'El, are you checking my pulse?' he asks. His face splits into a grin.

'I'm worried about you. Are you sure you're going to be okay? They haven't done their round yet. What if something's wrong?' My fingers are still holding his wrist, but I've lost count. It's soothing, though, feeling his pulse beneath his skin.

'Nothing will be wrong. And if there is something wrong, there are trained professionals here to fix it. Just go. I'll be fine.' He lifts his arm from my waist and rolls onto his back. I take a deep breath and push myself up off the bed. My body feels heavy. I don't want to go.

'Alright. But I'll just be down the street. Call me if anything happens.'

'Mm-hmm.' His eyes are shut and he's already falling back asleep. I run my fingers across his forehead again. Definitely too warm. I'll stop by the nurses' station on my way out.

I step outside the hospital doors and into the biting cold. Clouds swirl across the night sky, full and angry. As I cross the road, I feel the first spatter of rain.

Part IV

Theo

A nine-centimetre lump in my chest.

Hodgkin's lymphoma.

Survival rate – eighty per cent.

Relapse rate – ten to thirty per cent.

Enjoyment rate – zero per cent.

❦

I stare at the small plastic cup in my hand. It looks like a standard urine sample cup, except for the ominous black line marked around its circumference.

'We need you to fill to the line at least. Higher is ideal, if possible,' the nurse at the desk had said. She had followed this with a series of questions I hope to never be asked in public again.

I continue to stare at the cup, the cup that I have to jizz into and then hand to another human being. Rationally, I know it's totally okay and they handle this kind of thing every single day. Irrationally, I don't want to give my sperm to anyone. I want it stored, but I don't want to be part of the storing process. I wish I could come in, get it done and then leave the cup in the room. Honestly, I don't even want to do that, but it would be far better than the situation I'm in now.

I could've brought in a jizz sample from home, but when I thought about it, the logistics were just as awkward. Firstly, you have to get the jizz back to the clinic within an hour, which means I would have to alert my family to the fact that I had jacked off sometime in the previous sixty minutes, minus travel time. My family are close, but we aren't 'Hey son, how's your ejaculation collection going?' close. Then I would need to travel in a car with at least one of my parents (if not both because who doesn't want to come on a family adventure?) holding a cup of jizz.

I hadn't even thought about it when the doctor ran through the side effects of my treatment. But apparently Mum had. 'What does this mean for his fertility?' she had asked straight away. I'd nearly fallen off my chair. I'm not ready for kids. I'm twenty-four and just got told I have cancer. But more importantly, I don't want my mum talking about my dick!

'We will need a sperm sample before treatment begins, just in case,' the doctor had said. The 'just in case' had hung in the air. Mum nodded along like she was prepared to extract it herself. The woman is ready for grandchildren.

So now I'm standing in a room staring at this cup. This cup that I have to fill with sperm. Well, not fill, but catch it all because coming in to do it again is out of the question. How the fuck do I aim into a cup? Do I just pop the end of my dick into it? How am I meant to hold it steady? It's not exactly the same premise as just shoot and piss. I mean, you've got to hold the cup with one hand while jacking off with the other, while also making sure that nothing else gets into the cup that could contaminate the sample.

There's no clock in the room and I didn't check

the time when I came in, but I know I better hurry up and get it over with. I look around the room, properly taking it in for the first time. There's a chair, an old TV and DVD player on a trolley, and a stack of pornos sitting on the shelf underneath. I guess this is what I should've expected, but it doesn't make the task any easier. I just picture high school teachers dragging this same style TV trolley into classrooms for cringey PE and Science videos. Not exactly sexy.

I'll have to do it myself. Thank IBM for the invention of the smartphone. I pull mine out and get googling. And I'll have to do it standing. Again, rationally I know the chair is 'clean' but I can't stop thinking about how many arses have sat on it before me. I think of the sweat dripping off them and onto the faux leather. Stop thinking. Focus.

The air-conditioning keeps the room an even temperature, but goosebumps still dot their way across my arse. They haven't let me jizz for five days, to make sure I didn't run myself dry before today. It's a good idea in theory, but makes it feel like I'm going to explode, which adds to the anxiety about missing the cup. I make it quick, but not too quick. The whole time I imagine everything that could occur during: A fire. An earthquake. A terrorist attack. Someone bursting into the room. All would be equally bad in my anxiety-riddled mind.

I leave the room and stand at the front desk. The nurse doesn't notice me, so I give a little cough. I pass her the container and confirm my details are correct on the sticker she smooths along the front.

'All fine, enjoy the rest of your afternoon,' she says, like we've just had a completely normal transaction.

I wonder how much sperm she handles in a day. My palms are wet – fuck, I hope it's sweat. I need to get out of here.

*

The nurse comes in, dragging a machine and tray table behind him.

'Good evening,' he says to the room. 'How is everyone?'

I can't tell if it's rhetorical. Mum jumps right in. 'We're good, thank you.'

'Good to hear,' says the nurse. 'Theo, I'm just going to check your blood sugar, blood pressure and heart rate before we get started with the chemo today. If you could just sit up a bit for me, that would be great.'

I do as he asks and roll my sleeve up to make it easier for him. He stabs my finger and wipes the blood onto a little swatch, then shoves a clamp onto one of my other fingers. The screen lights up and the machine starts ticking away, the numbers rising. The nurse watches it, waiting for it to stop. He frowns at the screen.

'Theo, it's totally normal to be nervous. No-one looks forward to this. Are you anxious being here?' he asks. He knows it's a stupid question, but one that he has to ask. I don't give him shit for it. I bet people get angry or lie to him all the time.

'Yeah,' I say. 'I'm not gonna lie. I'm shitting bricks.'

'That's okay,' he reassures me. 'Your heart rate is a little high, but it might just be nerves.'

'What does this mean?' Mum interrupts.

'It's nothing to worry about for now. We'll keep an eye on it and keep checking it regularly. Theo, you tell us if you feel sick at any time, okay?' He smiles at me and then at Mum. Mum relaxes in her chair. Has he got sedatives in his smile? This nurse is a pro. I need him around next time I go toe-to-toe with Mum.

*

Chemo day one: check in at 11 a.m. Wait until 2 p.m. to get an IV. Wait until 3 p.m. to start treatment.

Chemo day two: wake up at 7 a.m. Can't eat breakfast. Lunch at 12 p.m. Can't eat lunch. Dinner at five-thirty. Can't eat dinner.

Chemo day three: repeat chemo day two.

Rest day one: sit at home, lie in bed.

Rest day two: repeat rest day one.

Chemo day four: repeat chemo day one. Sleep most of the time.

Chemo day five: repeat chemo day two.

Rest day three: released between 11 a.m. and 3 p.m. Go home.

Repeat. Repeat. Repeat.

*

My life is just a series of rounds. Rounds of blood tests, rounds of nurses, rounds of chemicals, rounds of rest. Round after round after round, only to come back to the same circumstances every time. 'Yes, you've still got cancer. Hodgkin's lymphoma, common for your age group and more common in males than females. Yes, the process is hard and slow. Yes, you'll need to come back in a fortnight. Yes, you need another round of treatment. Yes, there is always a chance it might come back.'

*

'Theo, we're going to have to cut down on your caffeine intake,' the doctor tells me. 'Your heart rate is still a little higher than we'd like it to be and we think it might be influenced by the coffee.'

Fuck.

'Cut it down by how much?'

'Eliminating caffeine from your diet would be ideal,' he says. I nod.

Why don't you just stab me in the heart? Would he notice if I ignored his advice?

'Looks like we'll be moving you onto warm milk,' Ella says from her seat next to my bed. 'You'll single-handedly keep the dairy industry profitable. It's a shame the coffee industry will be taking a huge dive though.'

She makes it better. She always makes it better.

*

I bolt up the stairs of my house taking them two at a time, busting for a piss. My fingers struggle with the fly on my jeans, fumbling. I used to be so coordinated. I long for a time when simple tasks are simple again. I'm going to have to sit, I don't trust myself to hold my dick and aim. I turn myself around and tug my pants down. When I pull my undies down, staring back at me are my pubes – not on my body but nestled together like a hairball in my undies. Honestly, it looks like all my pubes, too, every single one. The doctors didn't tell me my pubes would go too. They didn't even explicitly mention my pubes, just that I should be prepared for my hair to fall out. Which I was. But I forgot about my pubes.

I feel my balls. Soft, with just one or two stray, straggly hairs left. Should I pluck them out or just wait for them to fall off on their own? What if they don't fall off and I just have two fucking hairs on my balls? Not that anyone's going to be seeing my balls for a while. High libido is not one of the side effects of chemo as it turns out. Big surprise. What is definitely a side effect is the chemicals spreading their way so thoroughly through my body that I will likely sweat, salivate and jizz poison, which would be enough to put me off having sex with me. And that's not to mention the decline of self-esteem and sexual attraction now that I look like a cancer zombie. Think Voldemort's skin tone, with the under-eye circles of a raccoon and the weight distribution of Homer Simpson. Hot, right?

I look back at the hairs. What the fuck do I do with them? I don't want to leave them in my undies. I don't want to toss them in the bin – what if they fall out when Mum or Dad empty it? I can't wash them down the sink – a hairball like this would clog it up for sure. I stand carefully off the toilet and scoop them up, plucking out the extra hairs I missed with my free hand. I chuck them all into the toilet. They float in the piss-yellow water. I flush them away along with any hopes of having sex for the next twelve months.

*

'It's not something you'll likely need to consider very seriously, but you should think about the worst-case scenario. I recommend discussing, as a family, potential funeral arrangements,' the doctor says. 'As I said, your prospects are very promising and your treatment has a high success rate, but it's important to make sure everyone's wishes are clear.'

'Thank you,' we all murmur as he collects his clipboard and leaves. Mum and Dad look at one another. Ella stares straight ahead. I can see the tears building in the corners of her eyes, threatening to fall. She sits up a little straighter and closes her eyes.

When she opens them again, the tears have been pushed back inside.

'Well, that's an easy one to tick off,' Mum says. Her voice is chirpy and high-spirited. 'Not that we'll have to worry about it, though, since you're going to be just fine.' Mum has been facing the challenges with a positivity that rivals my own, but it feels forced and strained most days. Not to say that mine has come completely naturally. I wish she would be honest with her feelings. It would be easier for all of us. I don't know how to help her when she's like this.

'You'll have an Orthodox funeral, obviously,' she continues. 'But no point thinking about it now. Best to stay positive and keep our energy high.'

I know I should just let her think what she wants, but I can't let it slide this time.

'No, I won't,' I tell her. I can't keep the frustration out of my voice, but I bite back on the swear words. 'I'm an atheist.'

Mum's lips purse like she's eaten a lemon. She hates that word. 'I'm not changing it now just because I'm sick,' I say.

'You're Orthodox and you'll be having an Orthodox funeral,' she states again. Her voice slices through the air. Her hands rest in her lap, like the discussion is finished.

'No, I fuckin' won't. You're Orthodox. That doesn't mean I am. I'm an atheist and I'm not having any of that religious bullshit at my funeral.' I know it's because she's stressed and worried, and I know I should let it go, but I can't. Too many times she's ignored my opinions, cornered me at family gatherings with the priest, filled in my religion on the census. Too many times she's tried telling me what I am.

'Please respect my religion and heritage,' she says, her voice trembling. Dad stops watching the TV and looks at her. He's an atheist too.

'Tina,' Dad warns. He's watching Mum now, urging her not to pick this fight.

'Mum. This needs to be my decision, okay? I need you to not make this harder than it needs to be.'

I look at Ella and she looks down at her feet. Her right thumb is pressing its way across her left palm, rubbing away at the skin. She looks like she wants to be anywhere but here.

Mum moves to the end of my bed. Her eyes are glassy and wet. I take her hands in mine and we sit like this for a while. She is the first one to break the silence.

'I love you, Theo,' she says. 'I just want what I think is best for you.'

'I love you too,' I answer. 'I'll always love you.'

*

The nurses still ask if we have any questions, but there are none left to ask. We all shake our heads and wait for the next round of liquid to be attached and start pouring in. Ella always looks the saddest. She smiles whenever she notices me looking. But I can see it in her eyes. She has moulded her routine around me. She comes in after uni in the morning, bringing her readings or crochet. She sits quietly beside my parents, never heading out for coffee or leaving for a walk around the block. When my parents leave for dinner after watching me not eat mine, she moves herself onto the bed. She's become a pro at navigating the tubes and cords, working her way around them so she fits.

She snacks on biscuits I've saved for her and eats whatever she wants from my dinner. Sometimes she falls asleep. Mostly, she lies there waiting for me to want something. I try not to bother her, and just enjoy her body next to mine. The nurses let her stay until the announcement goes off at nine and sometimes the lenient ones let her stay a little longer. But eventually, she must disentangle herself from me, from the sheets, from the machinery, and make her way home.

*

'I love visiting the maternity ward,' Mum says. 'Those newborns fill my heart! Babies are so cute. I want to squish their little cheeks.' Mum is basically glowing. I know where this conversation will turn to next – my hypothetical babies. I watch Ella. She knows too. Her poker face doesn't change but I can tell she's uncomfortable. This is the third time Mum has mentioned the maternity ward and Ella hasn't responded. You'd think Mum would notice a pattern.

'Theo will make such a good dad,' Mum continues. Yep, there it is. Right on cue.

Ella doesn't want to be a mum. She's very happy with a corgi and some plants and that's about it. Her eyes flash wide at me. 'Save me', they scream. Ella knows Mum won't get it if she says she doesn't want kids.

'Mum, can we not talk about it?' I've been avoiding the conversation as much as Ella has. I'm not ready. I'm scared that I might want kids. I'm scared that I might want kids and Ella doesn't. I'm scared that we're going to go through all this for that to break us apart. I'm scared I might not even be able to have them after this anyway. The fears pile on top of one another, pressing down on my chest.

'Oh, Theo. It's going to be okay. You'll have plenty of time to make a family after this is all done.'

'Mum, please. I really don't wanna talk about it,' I say. I surprise us all when my voice catches. 'We don't even know if I'll be able to have kids. Probably got a dud dick and dud balls to match.'

The room goes quiet except for the low murmur of the TV. Dad continues to read in the corner.

'Sorry, sweet,' Mum says. 'Let me get you an extra blanket.' I look down the bed to where I already have three extra blankets piled, but I let her go anyway.

*

I cry when none of them are here. It's the only time I can cry. I smile from 11 a.m. when Mum gets in until Ella leaves at night. I try to be positive and hopeful. I talk about what I'm going to do when I get better and all of the things I'll achieve when I'm fully recovered. I'll get a job in architecture. Ella and I will buy a house. Mum sits proudly, listening to my stories, buying into all these dreams I have. But I don't count on anything anymore.

*

My bag is slung across my shoulder. I've stuffed it with my phone charger, toothbrush, mouthwash, chemo meds, steroid pills, nausea tablets, pain killers and a spare pair of undies. Everything else I can survive without. Mum and Dad sit in the lounge room in front of the TV. The news runs across the screen, but I don't think either of them are paying attention.

'Alright, I'm off. Love you guys,' I call out across the lounge room.

'Hold on,' calls Mum. 'Where are you going?'

'I'm staying at Ella's tonight.'

'How are you getting there?' Mum asks.

'Train,' I answer, like it's obvious. 'I'm not going to steal the car and drive it unlicensed, am I?' I don't mean to say it, but the steroids that are part of my therapy have hijacked my body. I imagine them coursing through me, a little army flicking at my nerves and tugging on my emotions.

'It's peak hour,' Dad replies.

'Yeah. So?' I wish they'd stop slowing me down. I'm already going to miss getting a seat; I don't want to be late as well. I know Ella wouldn't care, but she's making me dinner and I don't want to ruin that.

'The train is going to be full of germs,' Mum says.

'You're just being paranoid.' I can feel the steroids flowing through my blood and into my muscles. I am more conscious of their presence now. I recently declared that I was proud of how assertive I was becoming. Ella, Dad and Mum all exchanged glances before returning to reading and staring at the TV. Later that night, Ella gently took my hand and suggested that maybe what I felt was assertive was actually coming across as aggressive. She had said 'a little aggressive', but I know she was downplaying it to ease my guilt. It didn't help.

Mum and Dad look at one another. I'm not certain, but I get the feeling they might've been talking about me before I came in. They have a whole conversation without saying anything, before looking back at me.

'You can't catch the train,' Mum says.

Alright. So, she's decided to be the bad guy. Very well.

'It's safer for you to stay here, just in case. We can look after you here,' she continues.

'You think Ella won't look after me? Just because she doesn't do things exactly your way doesn't mean she can't do things.'

I know I sound like a brat, ungrateful and

uncaring. But I want just a little part of my normal life back and right now they're standing in the way of that. I want to see my girlfriend at her house. I want to have dinner with her and pretend for just a second that dating me is still easy. The steroids have won their battle and they're charging ahead in huge battalions.

'I didn't ask for you to look after me. I didn't ask you to burden yourselves with me – to sacrifice work, to become my live-in nurse or my security guards. I can still do things for myself.'

They look at each other again and Dad nods. He stands up from the lounge and starts walking over to me, before finally leaning against the wall beside me. His face is disappointed. I went too far. My face flushes with shame.

'Mate. You need to stay here,' he says. 'You can't just come and go as you please anymore. You need to be careful.' He's calm while he talks. He's always calm.

'I am careful.'

'You need to be smart too,' he says. 'No point doing all this if you're just going to go out and make yourself sick with something else. Getting a cold isn't the same for you anymore. Any infection could be life-threatening.'

'I'm not an idiot,' I tell him. But the fear seeps in and settles.

'Please? Do it for us. Ella will understand.'

I drop my bag to the floor and stomp up the stairs, slamming the door behind me. I sit on my bed and cry.

*

My piss is orange. Lolly orange. Mum, Dad and Ella join me in staring at the bowl before I flush. I haven't had anyone this interested in my piss since I was toilet training. I take a photo of it on my phone. There are very few highlights of the treatment, but this is definitely one of them.

*

The bed feels hard against my back, the blankets itch and the leggings are too tight. I roll over and over, trying to get comfortable without tangling myself in the IV line. I feel like a toddler on the verge of a tantrum. I know it's from the steroids and the lack of sleep, but that doesn't make it any better. I want to wrench the blankets off the bed, I want to kick my legs against the mattress, I want to rip the IV out of my arm. I stare up at the TV and ignore the new itch developing on my calf.

The room is quiet except for the murmur of the TV and the *tick-tick-tick* of the IV drip. It'll take ninety minutes for all of it to pulse into me. Then I'll get a short break, long enough to get up and piss or maybe go for a walk around the ward and then we'll go again for another thirty minutes. This is all followed by a dinner I won't be able to eat, a good session of dry-retching in the bathroom and three to ten hours of interrupted sleep. The whole thing will finish in four days. I'll have dark circles under my eyes, bruises speckled up my inner arm and scars along the back of my hand from when the veins in my arms could no longer accommodate the cannula.

*

'What time's Ella getting here?' Mum asks.

'Normal time.'

'She must be running late,' Dad says, checking his watch. 'We can grab lunch when she gets here.'

Dad likes Ella. They play the TV quiz shows together while I sleep. They'd make a mean pub trivia team. He knows old movies and history and she knows books and trashy 2000s music. Their blind spot would be geography, but I'm sure Dad could muddle through. Not Ella though – I'm still surprised when she can find Australia on a map. Absolutely no sense of direction or navigation in her.

I call her phone. No answer.

Hours pass. I sleep. I wait. Mum and Dad get lunch. Instead of eating in the cafe and taking their usual walk, they bring lunch back with them and eat in my room. I know they've both chosen plain sandwiches to reduce the lingering food smell. I call Ella again. And again.

Mum and Dad go home. I play the quiz shows by myself. I sleep.

She arrives after dinner. The nurses have already changed over.

'Where've you been?' My throat is tight. Is it from the chemo or my anxiety? I can never tell anymore. They all roll into one big churning stomach knot.

'I told you, I had a presentation today.' She tosses her bag onto the floor and drags the chair over to my bed.

'I've been worried all day. I told Mum and Dad you'd already be here. Why the hell didn't you tell me?' I sound aggressive. She's shocked, but I don't care. I feel tears prick my eyes.

'I did tell you.' Her hand sweeps across her forehead and she pushes her fingers into her temples. Fuck. I'm in for it now. How long has she looked this tired for? Have those bags under her eyes always been there? But I can't help it. I push on.

'No, you didn't. I would've known if you'd told me. You made me look stupid!' I slam my hand down on the bed. She jolts back a little. Her chair whines against the floor.

'Yes, I did,' she says, still calm, but slower this time. Quieter. She scrolls through her phone then turns her screen to me. 'I sent you a message to remind you. Look.'

I can't look. I know she must be right. A new bundle of anxiety adds itself to my stomach knot, rolling with the rest of my worries. 'I'm sorry,' I whisper. 'I forgot.'

How much have I forgotten? How much will I

continue to forget? Will it all come back when I'm done or is this as good as my memory will be? My biggest fear is the cancer coming back, but my second biggest fear is the forgetfulness staying.

She drags the chair closer to the bed. She is nearly touching me, her arm warm near mine. I don't want her to touch my hospital skin.

'You were meant to be here.' I sound like a child. Her hand brushes gently over my forehead. She takes my hand and slowly kisses each one of my fingers.

'I am here,' she says.

*

I sit on the lid of the toilet and roll down my compression socks. My calves jiggle as the fabric comes down and away from my legs. I hate the socks. I sit and let my legs breathe. They tingle as the temperature-controlled air flows across the hairs – the hairs I still have left, anyway. My legs look pale and depilated, like a plucked chicken. They're disgusting.

I turn on the shower and steam fills the tiny bathroom. I feel my muscles loosen. I roll my shoulders back and forward, trying to stretch out the tension. I thought they would be relaxed from all the rest and lying around, but they are tense and weak. I've never been this weak before. The smell of the hospital food makes my nausea worse and, when I can eat food at all, I can barely hold a spoon to my mouth without my wrist shaking. All I eat are hot chips and Minties. Everything tastes like metal, thanks to the poison that's meant to help me. I can't help but wonder if it's slowly killing me while it kills my cancer. They tell me it's not, but it doesn't feel like that.

I step into the shower and let the hot water wash over me. The steam mixes with my chemical sweat and the room smells sickly and stings my nose. I scrub the soap roughly across my skin, trying to scratch away the smell and the weakness. I wash until red marks pattern my body. I run my hands over my arms, my legs, my stomach. My muscles used to feel tight and strong under my skin. I was active and healthy – fat lot of good that did me. Now my muscles hide under layers of flab. I turn up the heat and let the hot water burn my skin.

I step out of the shower and stare at the stranger in the mirror. No dark curly hair, no clear skin, no smile. Just a lumpy bald scalp, with acne-scribbled skin and dark, almost-black bags under the eyes. Not exactly how I thought I'd look at twenty-five.

I sit back down on the lid of the toilet and try not to cry again.

*

The penultimate round is always the worst, the nurses keep telling us. I don't necessarily need them to tell me this. I can already feel it coming. The building sickness and anxiety as the minutes edge closer to my return to hospital. It's not the last round, so you know you'll have to do it all again, but it's not the first round, so you know what's coming and what it's going to feel like.

Like shit is what it feels like.

I know the nurses are trying to prepare me, to empathise with me, to support me. But it feels ominous and foreboding each time someone says, 'second-last round'.

My skin crawls when I smell the antibacterial gel. A wave of nausea rolls over me as I drag my feet across the tiles. My head feels faint as the nurses check me in. They tell me that it's totally normal, that it's my brain reacting to the pattern and the surroundings, a reaction to what is coming. They warn me that I'll probably experience heightened symptoms as my body copes with the treatment and the mental and bodily fatigue of the process at this later stage. They tell me that they see it all the time. We take the elevator to the tenth floor. We step up to the front desk, which is labelled 'oncology ward'. They know who I am. They ask how I've been, talk to Mum about her chickens and her nephew, talk to Dad about his crosswords and his classes. We ask how their kids are and how the weekend was. I wish we didn't know each other so well.

My fingers feel numb when they start bringing in the bags of chemicals that will soon be pumping through my body. I wonder if they will make a new bruise in my arm or if they'll just line it up on top of an existing one. I look at each tiny mark on my arm and feel the sting of each needle. My hands tremble, not from nerve damage as they initially thought, but from a genetic predisposition hidden inside me. Maybe stimulated by the treatment, but maybe not. Maybe triggered by caffeine, but maybe not. If I've learnt anything about medicine through this whole process, it's that there are a whole lot of maybes.

One thing is certain: the chemo nurse comes in wearing purple scrubs. I have grown to hate purple.

Part V

Theo and Ella

I keep checking the clock. I watch as 10 a.m. ticks by, then 10.30 a.m., then 11 a.m. I feel a rush of anxiety. Shit, I'm late. I need to get to the hospital. And then I remember. The cancer is like an old pet that has passed away; every once in a while I forget and think it's still there. I instinctively touch my chest where it used to be. At this same time a few months ago, I would have been sitting in my sterilised hospital room, waiting for the nurses to hook me up. Relief floods through my body.

I sit on the lounge at home with Ella and my parents, sipping my first post-treatment cup of coffee. It is black and steaming hot, burning my tongue slightly but worth it. Remission tastes good and I savour it.

Ella smiles and I'm so glad she's still here. She is relaxed with Mum and Dad now, and they with her. They have bonded while I have slept away these past months. Sometimes I wonder what they talked about during that time. Whenever I ask Ella, she shrugs and says 'Oh, you know ... stuff.' Though I'm still curious I don't press her. Part of me loves that they share something together, that something positive could come out of it all.

The clock ticks in the background and I remind myself to savour the things I can. I'm still in limbo, unable to fully jump back into my life, but this purgatory is better than the last.

*

People flow out of the doors of the Princess Theatre and into the crisp Melbourne air. Theo and I fall into step with the bodies around us. I stick close to his side, letting him lead me through the crowd. His fingers tremble in mine, a shake that may never fully go away. There are still so many uncertainties, things we will only know in time.

But there are some certainties too. For now, the cancer is gone. Treatment is over. We can kiss again. Theo's hair will never grow back into his dark Grecian curls. Each blood test for the next five years will fill us with dread and then relief, and there will always be a niggling part of both of us that worries they are wrong. We will always be cautious.

I look at Theo. His skin tone has slowly started to brown from the sun, no longer the yellow-white of chemo and fluorescent light. He's doing his best to adjust to life out of the hospital and back in the world. He's been learning how to eat with a spoon again, how to catch a ball again, how to write his signature. So many small and simple things no-one mentioned when talking about life after chemo. There are so many things the leaflets don't prepare you for.

Theo continues to weave his way through the tourists, couples posing for photos and bar-hoppers popping in and out of the pubs. We step across the pedestrian crossing and the crowd thins a little. I take it all in, being outside in the city with him, our first date night in over a year. As we continue to move towards Parliament Station, my fingers instinctively tighten in his. I have seen this station almost as many times as I have seen Theo in the last year. I know the exact number of steps from the top of the escalators to the doors of St Vincent's Hospital. It has been my daily commute, the platforms and carriages almost as familiar to me as my home. I have cried on these benches. I have daydreamed on these escalators. I have sat and waited and thought about our lives. These walls have held my fears, and my hopes.

But now it will hold new memories too. It is where Theo and I stand now, after our first date post-cancer.

His fingers squeeze mine before he lets go and then slips through the myki gate. He waits for me on the other side, standing near the top of the escalators. Our eyes meet and I still feel it, all this time later, the adoration he holds for me and I for him. I weave through the myki gate and meet him on the other side. He takes my fingers in his hand, lifts them to his lips and kisses my knuckles one by one.

So many things are different. We will never get that time back. But we're both still here, scarred, changed, but still breathing.

About the Author

Jacinta Dietrich is a writer and editor with a passion for sharing authentic stories. She holds a Master of Creative Writing, Publishing and Editing from The University of Melbourne. *This is Us Now* started life as her master's thesis and is her first published book. Jacinta is currently working on a middle-grade novel about a circus and siblings, and a young-adult novel about alchemy and family.

Author Acknowledgements

There are so many people who have helped me on the way to having this book published. Whether your contribution was big or small, I thank you. Sitting down to write this has made my heart full to bursting with love and gratitude. But the biggest thanks must go to the following people.

Firstly, my most heartfelt thanks to my partner Lucas. Without you there would be no story, for so many more reasons beyond the obvious. You have been a supporter since day one and have been ever so patient when I abandoned household tasks and adult life to jump into my books instead. Thank you for picking up the slack and giving me the time, space, food and coffee I needed to pull this off.

A huge thank you to my family. I have been reading and writing for almost as long as I can remember. That would never have happened without you reading to me, reading with me and buying me my next favourite book. You have all made me who I am today and I couldn't be more grateful. Special thanks to Mum for showing me how to be strong when everything goes to shit; to Tay for literally keeping me fed and clothed during one of the hardest periods of my life; and to Willow for teaching me patience and loving me despite all the bumps.

Thank you to Anna, David, Alana and Ash. Words can't express how grateful I am for all that we've shared, even the hard stuff. Thank you for your love, your kindness and for my place in your family. Your support (and word-of-mouth marketing) for this book was off the charts from the very start.

To my cheerleaders, Simon, Wes and Izzy. I would have run away screaming were you not on the other end of a text when the email came through. Thank you for your constant stream of praise, wisdom and reality checks. I would not have had the courage to share my writing without the excessive encouragement, tough love and gentle pushing from you three.

Thank you to my formative English teachers, Mary Spaeth, Dave Hanley and John Duncan, who pushed through all the terrible prose and poetry to help me uncover the good bits. Each of you helped me find my love for writing and that is the greatest gift you could have taught me. Of course, my deepest appreciation to Grace Yee, my thesis mentor. You saw the potential in this story when it was simply a speck of an idea. Without your guidance, it would never have become what it is today.

And my sincerest gratitude to the team at Grattan Street Press. To Katie and Sybil, thank you for seeing the value in my words and guiding me through the process so gently. You have validated my writing and taken the first stab at the imposter syndrome that lurks beneath. Thank you to all the students of Grattan Street Press. I know how hard you have all worked and I am so conscious of the fact that my book would not exist without your hours of blood, sweat, tears and passion. Your sensitivity, your kindness and your respect through the process has been so deeply felt and appreciated. I will never forget this experience and look forward to working with you all in the publishing industry in the near future. We will all be luckier for it.

Grattan Street Press Personnel

Semester 1, 2021

Editing and Proofreading:
Sophia Benjamin – Lead Copyeditor
Thirangie Jayatilake – Copyeditor
Lucinda Naughton – Copyeditor and Proofreader
Chloe Salecker – Chief Proofreader and Copyeditor
Aditya Sud – Copyeditor and Content Writer
Alana Tabacco – Proofreader and Sales and Marketing Officer

Design and Production:
Learncy Paul Kannan – Production Assistant and Proofreader
Timothy Smith – Production Manager
Poppy Willis – Production Assistant and Proofreader

Sales and Marketing:
Amelia Howell – Marketing and Publicity Officer and Content Writer
Olivia Jay – Publicity Manager
John Martin – Sales Manager
Sarah Strong – Events Manager
Alistair Trapnell – Marketing Manager

Social Media:

Tim Gauntlett – Social Media Editor and Scripts Editor

Submissions Officers:

Taylor Hay – Commissioning Editor and Proofreader
Daniel Holmes – Submissions Manager and Proofreader
Ian Dudley – Flash Fiction Submissions Manager
Frieda Hermann – Flash Fiction Submissions Manager and Proofreader
Sophie Raphael – Flash Fiction Submissions Manager

Website and Blogs:

Austin J. Ceravolo – MZ Co-editor
Jamisyn Gleeson – Book Reviews Editor, Proofreader and Sales and Marketing Officer
Marina Litchfield – Website Editor and Publishing Blog Editor
Jing Xuan Teo – MZ Co-editor

Academic Staff:

Sybil Nolan, Katherine Day, Alexandra Dane, Mark Davis.

About Grattan Street Press

Grattan Street Press is a trade publisher based in Melbourne. A start-up press, we aim to publish a range of work, including contemporary literature and trade non-fiction, and re-publish culturally valuable works that are out of print. The press is an initiative of the Publishing and Communications program in the School of Culture and Communication at The University of Melbourne and is staffed by graduate students, who receive hands-on experience of every aspect of the publication process.

The press is a not-for-profit organisation that seeks to build long-term relationships with the Australian literary and publishing community. We also partner with community organisations in Melbourne and beyond to co-publish books that contribute to public knowledge and discussion.

Organisations interested in partnering with us can contact us at coordinator@grattanstreetpress.com. Writers interested in submitting a manuscript to Grattan Street Press can contact us at editorial@grattanstreetpress.com.

Grattan Street Press Acknowledgement

After a year of running Grattan Street Press online, it was wonderful for our teaching press to return to on-campus operations in first semester, 2021. It was also wonderful to publish *This is Us Now*, Jacinta Dietrich's fine novella about a young couple living through the experience of cancer. We first published an extract from Jacinta's work in 2019 on our blog; bringing the finished book to readers has been a great pleasure for students and staff of the press. We believe it is not only an enjoyable read but also an important contribution to the narratives available for people – particularly people in their twenties and thirties, and their families – who suddenly find themselves landed with the devastating and completely unexpected news of a cancer diagnosis.

Jacinta has been a wonderful author to work with, not only because she's got a lovely way with words and knows how to tell a story, but also because of her wholehearted involvement in GSP's production of the book, from the editing stage through typesetting and proofing, and of course marketing. Throughout the experience, GSP students worked hard to make the book as great as it could be. The editing team, led by Sophia Benjamin, included Thirangie Jayatilake, Lucinda Naughton, Aditya Sud and Chloe Salecker, who also led the proofreading team, assisted there by Daniel Holmes, Taylor Hay, Frieda Hermann, Poppy Willis, Lucinda Naughton, Alana Tabacco and Jamisyn Gleeson. Timothy Smith produced a great concept for the book cover, and over several weeks it was brought to fruition with assistance from managing editor Katherine Day and others. Tim and Learncy Paul Kannan also typeset the book, based on a text design by our colleague and in-house book design expert Mark Davis. Poppy Willis was also part of the production team.

Throughout the semester we are always on the lookout for new and exciting texts to publish and our submissions editors Daniel Holmes and Taylor Hay spent many hours reading and assessing manuscripts. Ian Dudley, Sophie Raphael and Frieda Hermann also assessed and gathered a fine collection of works for our next publication (coming soon!).

The marketing team, led by Alistair Trapnell, and including Olivia Jay, Tim Gauntlett, Amelia Howell and Sarah Strong, did a great job of getting the word out about Jacinta and her book on social media and through media releases. The beautiful author headshots we have used in the book and our publicity were courtesy of Simon McCarthy. The website team, led by Marina Litchfield, promoted the book through an author interview and other coverage. Austin Ceravolo and Jing Xuan Teo commissioned and edited a selection of thought-provoking posts about the lives and concerns of Millennials and Gen Zs for our MZ blog. Jamisyn Gleeson started GSP's online book review section, which will further strengthen our links to Melbourne's vibrant literary scene by reviewing books published by other Australian publishers, large and small.

Unfortunately, COVID-19 left the book industry with an unwanted legacy. Bookselling was initially knocked off balance by long lockdowns. In its usual way, the Australian industry regrouped and went on to have strong sales in 2020 but for many bookstores approaches to ordering stock have necessarily changed. This has made it more challenging than ever before for small presses to have their books stocked in bricks-and-mortar bookshops. The sales team this semester, John Martin and Alana Tabacco, had to work within this new context. We are grateful to the independent bookstores who have continued to support GSP's work by stocking our titles.

In the Master of Publishing and Communications program, a heartfelt thanks to colleagues who have continued to support GSP's work during an extraordinarily busy year: our program coordinator Alex Dane (who is also GSP's digital publisher), Mark Davis, Beth Driscoll, Susannah Bowen, Kenna MacTavish and particularly Katherine Day, who has been a stalwart of the GSP team.

Thanks to our new Head of School, Assoc. Professor Paul Rae, who has been so supportive of GSP this semester; also to his EA, Jacqueline Doyle, and to our School Manager, Charlotte Morgans, who both gave assistance that kept the administrative wheels turning. Thanks also to Kerin Forstmanis, who has supported GSP regarding contract matters for several years now. And last but not least thanks to IngramSpark, who always come through for us on the printing front.

Sybil Nolan
Publisher at Grattan Street Press

www.ingramcontent.com/pod-product-compliance
Ingram Content Group Australia Pty Ltd
76 Discovery Rd, Dandenong South VIC 3175, AU
AUHW010631050325
407891AU00003B/19